THE UNICORN AND THE PLOW

by Louise Moeri

illustrated by Diane Goode

E. P. DUTTON · NEW YORK

Text copyright © 1982 by Louise Moeri
Illustrations copyright © 1982 by Diane Goode

Library of Congress Cataloging in Publication Data

Moeri, Louise.   The unicorn and the plow.
Summary: A poor starving farmer is persuaded by his two
oxen to wait one more day before he sells one and kills
the other for food.
[1. Fairy tales.   2. Unicorns–Fiction]
I. Goode, Diane, ill.   II. Title.
PZ8.M717Un   1982   [E]   81-15287
ISBN 0-525-45116-1   AACR2

Published in the United States by E. P. Dutton, Inc.,
2 Park Avenue, New York, N.Y. 10016

Published simultaneously in Canada by Clarke,
Irwin & Company Limited, Toronto and Vancouver

Editor: Ann Durell   Designer: Claire Counihan

Printed in the U.S.A.   First Edition
10 9 8 7 6 5 4 3 2 1

to my grandson
Nathaniel Moeri
L.M.

to Michael Capuozzo
D.G.

There was once a man who lived on a tiny farm at the edge of a dark forest. Every day he went out with his oxen and his plow and tilled the small fields and cleared them of rank green weeds. But every day the weeds sprang up again. It seemed they bloomed, set seed, and sprouted again right behind the plow. No matter how hard the farmer worked, his crops could not prosper. Although he took loving care of his oxen, sharpened his plowshares daily, and kept a welcoming house for both friends and wayfarers, he grew poorer year by year.

At last, after endless struggle with the barren fields, the farmer had nothing save his oxen, and he went out one day with an axe in his hand to kill one of them to eat.

"Oh, poor beasts," he said to the two heavy, patient oxen, "you have served me well. It breaks my heart to part with you, but I am starving. So I must sell one of you, and slaughter the other to eat." And he raised his axe to strike.

Suddenly one of the oxen—the black one—spoke: "Master—Master—wait— Do not harm us! Wait one more day— Help will come to you if you spare us."

The farmer was astounded. He had plowed and harrowed every day for years with the animals and never guessed that they could speak. "What?" he cried. "Why did you never speak before?"

"The need was never so great before," said the black ox. "But the time has come for miracles."

"Miracles! Ha!" cried the farmer bitterly. "Miracles, indeed! Do you see any miracles around here, Ox?"

Quite forgetting, in his despair, the remarkable fact that his ox was speaking, he gestured at the little thatched hut, with its broken windows and sagging door, the byre empty of hay, and the small fields choked with rank green weeds.

"Oh, no, Master—but it's only when things are at their very worst that miracles occur," said the white ox. "Wait one more day, and see what happens."

So the farmer laid down the axe. There was no hay, so he could not feed the oxen, but he gathered leaves from the birch trees at the edge of the forest for them to eat, and cooked himself a pot of nettles. "Never cared much for nettles," he grumbled, as he stirred the pot.

"Wait," said the black ox as he ate his birch leaves.

"Wait," said the white ox.

The farmer waited. At noontime he was hungry again, but he had eaten all the nettles for breakfast.

"I'll try to snare some game," he said as he took down his net. He went a short way into the forest and sat down in a thicket to wait for a rabbit. He was so hungry that his stomach growled and talked to itself.

"Empty. Empty. Empty," his stomach muttered.

"Quiet," said the farmer. "You'll scare away the rabbits."

Suddenly the farmer caught his breath. There, just outside the thicket, was a big gray rabbit. The rabbit had seen him, but she did not run away. Carefully, carefully, the farmer raised his net. But just as he was ready to cast it, he looked down. There at his feet was the rabbit's burrow, with a tiny rabbit peeping out.

The farmer let the net fall. "Come to think of it—I'm not that hungry yet. I'll just go see if I can find some more nettles," he told his stomach. "A little one needs its mother, and I never cared much for rabbit anyway."

By evening the farmer was hungrier than ever, and very tired of eating stewed nettles. He decided to see if he could find a bird's nest with eggs in it for his supper. So he brought the oxen to stand under the oak tree beside the hut, and he climbed up on their backs and into the tree.

Sure enough, there was a nest, and near it perched a mockingbird. In the nest were three lovely eggs. The farmer crept out on the limb, further and further, and he was just about to seize the eggs when the mockingbird began to sing.

The farmer jerked back his hand. "Oh," he cried, "if I take those eggs, they won't hatch and the birds won't grow up to sing. And the world needs mockingbirds."

So the farmer carefully crept back along the limb, dropped down onto the oxen's backs, and so to the ground. "Nettles for supper again," he sighed, "and I'll just see if I can find some more birch leaves for you."

So the farmer gathered more nettles and more leaves, and at last both he and the oxen were fed.

When darkness fell that night, he went out to put the oxen in their byre. "Well, beasts," he said to them, "you told me to wait for miracles. I have waited all day, and no miracle has happened. It seems you were wrong."

"Are you sorry you spared us?" asked the black ox.

The farmer thought a moment. "No," he said.

"Are you sorry you spared the rabbit and the mockingbird eggs?" asked the white ox.

"No."

"Then wait," said the beasts.

So the farmer stabled the oxen in the byre and went back to the hut to sleep. He was very tired, so he fell asleep at once, although he was still hungry. But he woke again when the moon rose.

As he opened his eyes, he saw the light cast by the moon glowing through the window of the hut so brilliantly that it dazzled him. "Surely this is a remarkably bright moon," he said, "to cast such a light. Why, it's as bright as the sun. I'll just get up and look out."

He crept out of bed and pulled on his clothes and went out of the hut to look around.

And what a sight met his eyes! There, in the field closest to the hut, was his plow—turning deep furrows and cutting out the cruel green weeds. And the plow was pulled by a unicorn!

The farmer clapped his hands to his head. He was so surprised that he wanted to laugh and shout, but he could not make a single sound. All he could do was dance up and down and watch the little silvery unicorn as it floated effortlessly around and around the field, pulling the plow through the black, black soil. The weeds shriveled at the touch of the plowshare, curled over and died, and the farmer could see that the field had never looked so rich, so fertile.

All night long by the light of the moon, the
unicorn plowed the fields. Every furrow was straight
as a moonbeam, though now and then, just for fun,
the unicorn plowed a great scroll or curlicue that
looked like the carving on a castle or a cathedral.

At last the work was done. Just as the moon set
behind the forest, the last furrow was plowed, and in
each furrow there now appeared the green leaves of
a vast crop—turnips, corn, cucumbers and pump-
kins! In the blink of an eye, the unicorn stepped out
of the traces, left the plow and galloped away,
vanishing into the dark forest.

When day dawned, the farmer, who had recovered his speech the moment the unicorn galloped off, raced to the byre to tell the oxen what had happened.

"Black Ox! White Ox! You were right— Just when everything seemed hopeless, you told me not to give up. And the miracle has happened! A unicorn came last night and plowed the fields—now there isn't a weed in sight!"

"And, oh, what a crop of vegetables has sprung up–" he continued. "Come out and see!" He led the oxen from the byre. "Now," cried the farmer as he showed them the fields, "tell me what you think of that!"

The black ox looked. The white ox looked. And then, just as the mockingbird began to sing, they nodded their heads and spoke.

"M-m-m-m-m-moooooooooo–" they said.